"KNOCK, KNOCK! TRICK OR TREAT?"

A Haunting Fable-within-Fable for the Costume Enabled of
Gluttonous Fools & Ghastly Ghouls

Written & Designed by Ron Roecker

"Ron's books are delightfully creative."
Jodi Murphy, Co-Founder, Geek Club Books for Autism

"They're calling him the next Mr. Rogers! Ron Roecker's inspirational
books and positive messages are exactly what we all need right now."
Leeza Gibbons, Emmy-winner, NY Times Best-Selling Author

Also Available at Amazon Worldwide by Ron Roecker:

MONSTER DEDICATIONS:

To Grandma Mohney and everyone who was able to experience her "Costume Room," which was open all year long! It was magical, and so was she!

To anyone clever enough to DIY a really amazing costume.

Families that dress in themed costumes.

To Lisa C – you had me at "Pat." Llllllllove you.

Each Halloween with "Trick or Treat?"
When costumed monsters come to meet,
Is measured by how much they hoard,
While selling souls from door-to-door.

For candy corn and caramel rats,
Marshmallow ghosts and chocolate bats,
Sour snakes and gummy scars,
The Holy Grail? A full-sized bar!

Ghastly ghosts in hand-me-down sheets,
Pal princesses with rhinestoned feet,
Naughty ninjas with swords of foam,

Some costumes are bought
and some are hand-sewn.

But now, dear friends, the lessons start.
There's no façade for one's true heart.
Let us now watch this gluttonous soul.
Will he be one for whom doorbells toll?

As night turns black with rotting mist
The others leave but you persist.
At midnight then you see the last door.
"I'll have it all when there is no more!"

You walk onto the creaking porch.
The path is lit by cobwebbed torch.
You knock, knock, knock to get just sweets.
But now things turn more trick than treat.

For all the day the undead played,
Within their house of life's decay,
Insanely waiting for your knock,
Upon the doors you hear unlock.

The house itself now begs you in,
as frantic shivers stab your skin.
You clear your throat, "Um, Trick or Tr…"
As something slithers 'neath your feet.

You stumble down the stairs to Hell
Then crash into a bloody well,
With bones and eyes of gobbled guests,
As tattered hang the drapes of flesh.

Then darkened tones from nowhere play.
You try to keep werewolves at bay.
The smell of evil by your side
Your human flesh you cannot hide.

Then suddenly, you're off the ground.
You float in place, now gagged and bound.
You've fallen prey to ghastly ghouls
Who scream at you like maddened fools:

"*Knock, knock, Dear One, in stark denial,*
Alas tonight must stand on trial.
For mortal ones we all abhor
Must pay for knocking on our door.

With hair of mange and lizard tongue,
Add Bullfrog bile and Satan's lung,
A pinch of poison ...never first;
For it will end eternal thirst."

"Now drink your bubbly brew of foam.
We haunt to make you feel at home.
There, there, my dear, why do you cry?
You think you'll not live once you die?
You'll live, my love, among us all,
The great Undead who live for Fall!"

And as you hear these final words,
They leap upon in evil herds,
Depriving you of soul and air,
You watch them feast but cannot care.

You think of all the wicked treats
You always knew you'd never eat.
Such foolish thinking: *more is more*
You had to knock on one last door!

Then suddenly you now belong,
For mortal death is what you long.

And nothing ends
Your *madness* more,
Than next year's *knock*
Upon the door.

(spooky laughter)

Oh, what an end
you're white as my aunt.
Do you need a hug?
Oh, wait, I can't.
Is this tale, um,
hypothetical?
Any truth would
be heretical.

Unlike our ghost
This tale has an end.
(This must be shared
again and again…)

Learn from this tale,
(poor, undead ghost):
Those who *want* more
don't *need* the most.

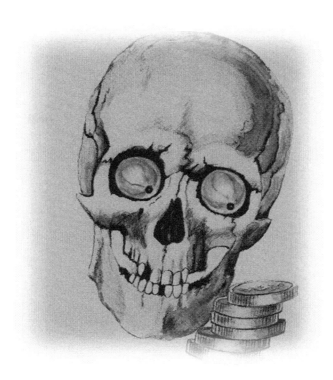

Halloween
is haunted by fools,
They want it all
except the rules.
The unsatisfied
miss the bar,
Not quite enough
or, oops, too far.

For all the fools,
here is a reminder,
To make Halloween
Sweeter and Kinder:

"Trick or Treat?"
is not rhetorical,
"Trick or Treat?"
is not metaphorical.

The one who chooses
"Trick or Treat?"
Answers the door,
(the one you meet).

You do not choose,
but you implore,
Your fate awaits
behind each door.

Selling your soul,
hedging your bets
Only will net you
eternal debt.

Live a rich life
and get what you need.
The trick to life's treats
is all that you heed.

Take what you will
from our little story
(hey, we're monsters,
it had to get gory).

If there is one thing
We hope you will save
Is this living lesson,
we'll take to the grave:

When you get the feeling,
that craving for more,
Just make sure you stop
at the next-to-last door.

The End

Also available by Ron Roecker at Amazon Worldwide:

Amazon   Kindle   GoodReads   LitPick   Reedsy Discovery

BookAuthority.org   Prairies Book Review   OnlineBookClub.com

To book an Author Meet-and-Read event via Zoom for your classrooms, send an email to ronwroteit@gmail.com

www.facebook.com/ronwroteit

Made in the USA
Middletown, DE
02 October 2021